SPIRIT CHILD

• SeaStar Books •

New York

SPIRIT CHILD
A STORY OF THE
NATIVITY

Translated from the Aztec by
JOHN BIERHORST
Pictures by
BARBARA COONEY

Text copyright © 1984 by John Bierhorst
Illustrations copyright © 1984 by Barbara Cooney
First published by William Morrow and Company, New York, 1984.

SEASTAR BOOKS
A division of NORTH-SOUTH BOOKS INC.

Published in the United States by SeaStar Books,
a division of North-South Books Inc., New York.
Published simultaneously in Canada, Australia, and New Zealand
by North-South Books, an imprint of Nord-Süd Verlag AG,
Gossau Zürich, Switzerland.

Library of Congress Cataloging-in-Publication Data is available.
The artwork for this book was prepared by using gouache.
Designed by Jane Byers Bierhorst

ISBN 1-58717-087-6 (reinforced trade binding)
1 3 5 7 9 RT 10 8 6 4 2
ISBN 1-58717-088-4 (paperback binding)
1 3 5 7 9 PB 10 8 6 4 2

Printed in Hong Kong

For more information about our books,
and the authors and artists who create them, visit our
web site: www.northsouth.com

SPIRIT CHILD

For five thousand years after the world began, the devil was king. He was proud and mean, and there was no one anywhere on earth who could save us from his hands.

Many people had been born who were strong and intelligent and who lived good lives, but they did not have the power to save either themselves or anyone else from the hands of the devil.

The devil is clever. While we are alive on earth, he never shows us how many terrible things he will do to us later. While he laughs, he closes our eyes and makes us blind. Then he takes us away to the Dead Land.

In the Dead Land, there is nothing but hunger and arguments all the time, and sickness, and hard work.

But the name Jesus already existed before the world began. This was always his name, even before he was born. When he came to earth, the thing that he did was to save people from the devil. And just like the thing that he did, so was his name, because the word Jesus means savior of people.

O spirit, O child, you are the flame, you are the light of the almighty father. O child, remember how you were born long ago.

There was a certain Joseph who was very wise and whose heart was good. It was he who married the young woman who was to become the mother of the spirit. And yet, though married, she remained a young unmarried woman. Joseph, too, though married, remained a young bachelor. He never really stopped being a boy.

When Joseph and Mary had been joined in this miraculous way, the lord God sent his messenger, the angel Gabriel. Down he came to the country of Galilee, to the city called Nazareth.

When he found the house where the young woman was

living, he came in and stood beside her and spoke these holy words: "Hail Mary, full of grace, God is with you.

"O lady, you are blessed, you are worthy in God's eyes. You are the most fortunate of women. God has favored you. He has filled your soul with the power of life, and because of this you will be praised in all the world."

But when Mary heard these words she was troubled. She did not think she was worthy of the angel's greeting, because she was very meek. She began to reflect on it, thinking about the angel's message. Then she said, "Why should someone talk to me like this? Why should I be praised?"

The angel Gabriel's face came shining, the way the sun comes up making everything bright. His wings came gleaming, came glistening. They were longer and more brilliantly green than quetzal plumes.

Now the angel said to the lady, "O Mary, don't be afraid. You are praised in God's eyes.

"Listen! I will tell you a great mystery. A child will be established inside your womb. You will conceive. And the child will be called Jesus.

"This boy of yours, this Jesus, will be very great. He will rule the kingdom of David, and his rule will never end."

But when the lady had heard the angel, she said, "How can this be done, for I do not know a man?"

"The power of God, the holy spirit, will come over you," said the angel. "And because of this a child will be born who will be perfectly good, who will be called the son of God."

"Here I am," said Mary. "I am the servant of the lord. Let it be done to me just as you have said."

At that moment our lord God, God the son, became a human being inside the womb of the lady Mary, the perfect young woman. At that moment the lady Mary became the mother of God.

The angel appeared to Joseph and said, "Joseph, I will tell you a mystery. Mary has been made pregnant by the holy spirit. Do not be afraid. Stay with her. She will give birth to the savior of the world."

Then Joseph became Mary's guardian. He took her with him everywhere he went. He protected her and was always at her side. They lived together, they ate together.

God the father had chosen Joseph to be the guardian of his child because Joseph was more good-hearted than other people in the world. So Joseph became God's servant, the one who took care of God's child.

Because of a command issued by Caesar, Joseph had to
go to Bethlehem, and he took Mary with him. Now the
days had been accomplished for her to give birth to
her baby.

O spirit child! All the people of the world are waiting
for you. We are prisoners tied in chains, and you can save
us. You are the light, and we are in darkness. Come soon,
come keep your promise.

O sacred king of Jerusalem, O sacred prince, O noble
child, wake up! Be alive! The skies will be glad, and the
earth will dance.

When Mary reached Bethlehem with Joseph, and the number of her days had been accomplished, she gave birth to her baby, her firstborn child.

When her baby was born, she wrapped him in a cloth and laid him in a manger, a place where cows eat dry grass.

This savior of ours only needed a little dry grass for his bed, he did not hate to be in the manger, and his heart was content with a very small amount of food.

When King Jesus was born, it was nighttime. Yet the young woman Mary, holding her baby, saw the sun in the sky. Then she knelt and worshipped the baby, for this was a sign that a great king had come to earth.

Everywhere in the world a great many miracles were made when our lord Jesus Christ was born.

When the sun in the sky, which is Jesus, appeared that night, it was three suns. People were amazed. Then again the three suns in the sky became one.

It was the middle of the night when the spirit child Jesus was born. Yet everywhere in the world it became light.

When our lord Jesus was born, a fountain of sweet oil

appeared in Rome. It was a sign that all people who worshipped idols and false gods would be forgiven.

When our ruler Jesus was born, the grapevines miraculously blossomed in Jerusalem at a place called Engedi. It was a sign that the devil's teaching would be destroyed.

When the noble child Jesus our ruler, called king of peace, arrived, there was suddenly peace in all the world.

Now on the outskirts of Bethlehem there were shepherds watching their sheep by night. The angel Gabriel appeared to them, and a great light from heaven came down.

The angel said, "O friends, I come to tell you great words. Today in Bethlehem a savior has been born. His name is Jesus.

"Go to Bethlehem. There you will find him, in the
city of David. Alleluia, alleluia."

Then many angels appeared, singing their mysterious
word, alleluia, praising the child who was born king.

Shepherds, tell us. Did you see him?

"We definitely saw him."

How did you find him?

"We heard the angels singing."

The angels came down from the sky like birds. Their voices were bells. They sounded like flutes. "Praise God in heaven, alleluia."

They came flying out of the sky, singing, "Peace on earth, alleluia."

Sweet-smelling song-flowers were scattering everywhere, falling to earth in a golden rain. "Let's scatter these golden flowers, alleluia."

The flowers are heavy with dew, and the dew is filled with light, shining like jewels in Bethlehem. "Alleluia."

Heart flowers, plumelike bell flowers, red cup flowers. They're beaming with dawn light, they're shining like gold. "Alleluia."

Emeralds, pearls, and red crystals are glowing. They're glistening. It's dawn. "Alleluia."

Jewels are spilling in Bethlehem, falling to earth. "Alleluia."

When Jesus was born in Bethlehem a new star appeared
in the sky. It had been said that a star would be born out
of Jacob, and people had waited a long time. The prophet
had said, "A man will arise, he will be born out of Israel.
A savior will be born in Judea. Then a new star will appear."

People were watching. When they saw the star, they
told their kings. And so the three kings came out of the
east. Guided by the star, they traveled toward Bethlehem.

They came carrying myrrh, incense, and gold. "Where

is he that was born king of the Jews?" they asked.

When they got to Jerusalem, they questioned people. "Where is the ruler? Where is the king?"

When Herod, the ruler of Judea, heard that people had come looking for a new king, he was jealous. He summoned the chief priests of Jerusalem and asked them, "Where is this king, this Christ that people have been waiting for?"

"In Bethlehem," they said, "which is part of Judea."

When Herod heard the news, he secretly summoned the three kings and questioned them very carefully about the star, asking them when they had first seen it.

The three kings told him everything. Then Herod said, "Go on to Bethlehem. When you have found the child, come back and let me hear about it. I want to worship him, too."

But Herod was not telling the truth. He craftily said to the three kings, "Oh yes, I will go adore the true king who has arrived on earth. I will go greet him and make him my god." But he only wanted to kill the child Jesus.

When the kings had heard what Herod had to say, they went straight to Bethlehem.

And again here it is, the star that they had seen before. It shone down on them and made them glad, because when they had come into Jerusalem the walls of the city had blotted it out.

Again the star guided them, and the kings watched it as they traveled along. When they got to Bethlehem, the star rested over the stable where the child lay.

Well now, they entered the building. And so these kings who had seen the star, who stirred no more, who traveled no more, came and knew him, for he was there. They entered the stable and saw the child Jesus and his precious mother, holy Mary.

They fell prostrate and adored the child. As believers, these great kings knelt and adored him. They recognized this little child. For he is the spirit, he is all powerful, he is sky owner, he is earth owner.

They opened their coffers, their chests. Then they laid things before their lord, presenting things to the child.

The offering that they made was gold, myrrh, and incense.

Well then, for a few days they remained at the child's side, and many marvels did they see. Then in their sleep they were commanded to go away. They saw the spirit child in their sleep. They dreamed him, and in this way he sent them directly home.

They did not return to Herod, because the spirit child knew what Herod wanted to do.

O evil Herod! Can you fool the Almighty? Though he is only a child, a baby, Jesus knows everything, for he is God.

His holiness and mysteriousness are exactly the same as the holiness and mysteriousness of God the father himself. It is God the father who has become a human being and has come to live among us.

He has come to be our savior. Everyone can be spared. The devil has no power to seize even a single person from the hands of Jesus.

Now a heavenly peace has come over the earth. Now everywhere in the world a beautiful rain, a wonderful rain is falling. A miraculous rain has come over the earth.

Now this is the day of salvation that was long awaited. It shines on us, it lights our way.

Note

The story of spirit child was recited by Aztec chanters to the accompaniment of the upright skin-drum called *huehuetl* and the two-toned log drum called *teponaztli*. Composed by the missionary Fray Bernardino de Sahagún, who had the assistance of Aztec poets, it combines stories from the Bible, medieval legends, and traditional Aztec lore. Clearly the basic material comes from the gospels of Matthew and Luke. Various details, such as the description of the devil and the mention of miracles that occurred on the night of Christ's birth, appear to be drawn from European folklore. Yet the manner in which the story unfolds, with its short paragraphs, its dialogue, and its way of addressing main characters directly, is very much in the Aztec tradition. Several passages, including the angels' song to the shepherds, even use Aztec figures of speech. The story is preserved in Sahagún's *Psalmodia Christiana* (Mexico, 1583), a book written entirely in the Aztec language and one of the first books published in the New World. The present translation, the first in any modern language, has been made from a microfilm of the *Psalmodia* taken from a copy of the book itself in the John Carter Brown Library at Brown University. The folio numbers of the passages from which this version has been made are 16v-17v, 18v-23v, 48v-49v, 51v-57v, and 230v-236.

This book ~~belongs to:~~
is shared with

_____

_____

_____

the elephant who
tried to tiptoe

to all who wobble

© 2016 Conscious Stories LLC

Illustrations by Liesl Bell

Published by
Conscious Stories LLC

www.consciousstories.com

First Edition
ISBN 978-1-943750-02-3
Printed in China

1 2 3 4 5 6 7 8 9 10

Dear parents, teachers and readers

This story has been gift-wrapped with two simple mindfulness practices to help you connect more deeply with your children in the last 20 minutes of each day.

● Quietly set your intention for calm and open connection.

● Then start your story time with the **Snuggle Breathing Meditation**. Read each line aloud and take slow deep breaths together. This can be very relaxing and help everyone settle.

● At the end of the story you will find **Ellie's Bedtime Body Scan**. This will help your little ones relax as they connect with different parts of their body. You can rest a hand on each part as you help them to relax and slow their breathing. Some parents do a short massage to help their children settle.

Enjoy Snuggling into Togetherness!

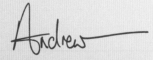

Snuggle Breathing

Our story begins with us breathing together.
Say each line aloud and then
take a slow deep breath in and out.

I breathe for me

I breathe for you

I breathe for us

I breathe for all that surrounds us

The body I've been given
Is a big grey heavy one;
It isn't light like fairies,
Nor fast, like cheetahs run.

It's not a very small one
Like the tiny mouse;
It doesn't flap with feathers
Or have an indoor house.

My body doesn't stand
On tiptoes very well;
My feet can't hold bananas;
My mouth can't squawk or spell.

I can't catch fish with paws
Or swing from tree to tree;
I sometimes wish I could –
But that just isn't me!

Those are special features
Of others in the wild;
Each is quite unique
Like every special child.

I have some special features
of my very own.
I was born an elephant –
I wander and I roam.

SPECIAL FEATURES

15

I have a herd who loves me;
A nose that's supercool;
The biggest ears you've ever seen
And in the wild, I rule!

17

My nature is so gentle
Despite my giant size;
My memory is excellent and
I have very pretty eyes.

19

My body is my body;

It is my own to rule;

It has some kinks and wobbles.

I think it's supercool!

When I do remember
To be my own true self;
Not tiptoe or try flying
Or hiding like an elf...

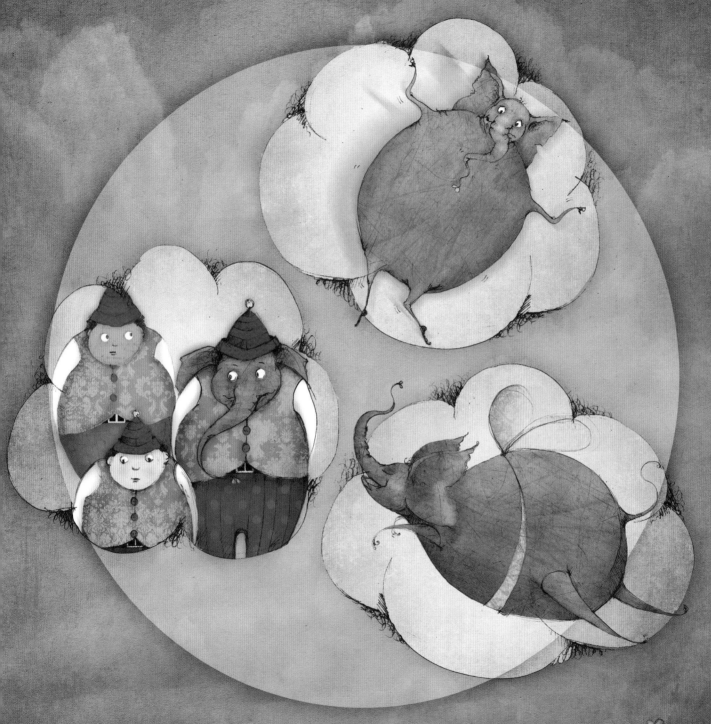

Then I am most happy;
Most playful and most free;
Doing what I love to do...

Being truly me.

Do you know?

How to hide an elephant

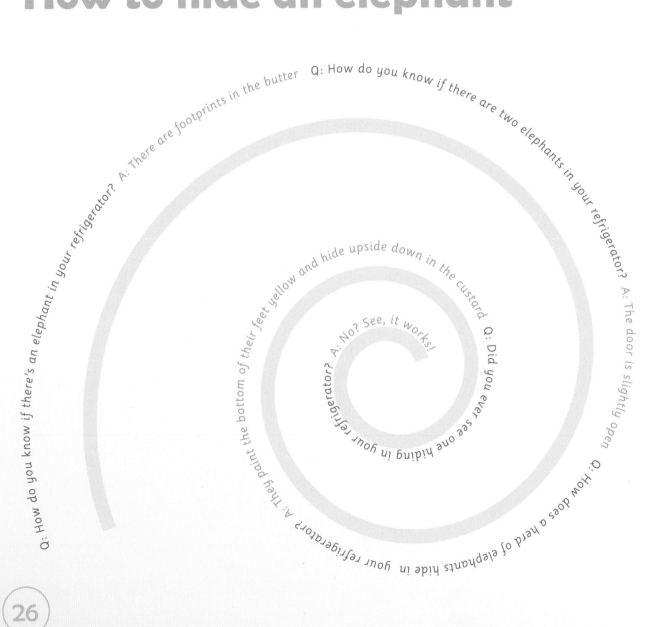

Q: How do you know if there's an elephant in your refrigerator? A: There are footprints in the butter   Q: How do you know if there are two elephants in your refrigerator?   A: The door is slightly open   Q: How does a herd of elephants hide in your refrigerator?   A: They paint the bottom of their feet yellow and hide upside down in the custard   Q: Did you ever see one hiding in your refrigerator?   A: No? See, it works!

26

A relaxing exercise
Ellie's Body Scan

Let out sigh;
It's soon goodbye.

4 AAAH...

Big breath in;
Let's begin:

2

3

Squeeze eyes tight;
Prepare for night.

SQUEEZE

5

Squeeze your knees;
Let go with ease.

1

Wriggle toes;
Scrunchle nose.

Do this exercise with me for a great sleep...

Drum your heart;
Slow to start.

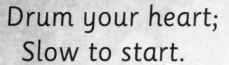

Close eyes tight;
Squeeze with might.

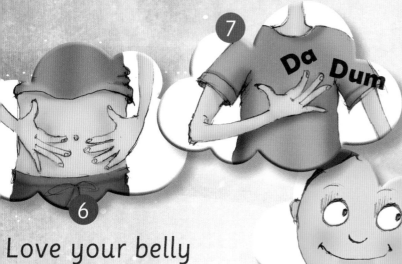

Love your belly
Just like Ellie!

Make a smile
For a while.

Let out sigh;
Say goodbye.

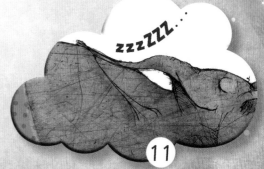

Night night; Sleep tight.

the prayer who searched for god

Coming Soon

tor silence

Andrew Newman

the laughing witch

Andrew Newman

the fish who nearly drowned in his search for water

the elephant who tried to tiptoe

the dad who didn't know

Andrew Newman

the hug who got stuck

the collection

The Conscious Bedtime Story Club

snuggling into togetherness

the forgetful elephant

Andrew Newman

a little light

the tree of goodness

Andrew Newman

the circle people

Coming Soon

Andrew Newman

the bee who could not choose a flower

Andrew Newman

what the club offers

A collection of stories with wise and lovable characters who teach spiritual values to your children

Delivered straight to your home over the course of one year.

One whole year of bedtime stories

Meet wonderful heroic characters with big hearts and deep values as they encounter exciting challenges and move towards freedom.

Simple mindfulness practices

Enjoy easy breathing practices that soften the atmosphere and create deep connection when reading together.

Create your own story books

Unleash your creativity by writing and coloring your own stories.

Reflective activity pages

Open sharing time with your children at the end of each day.

Delivered to your home

Make one decision today and experience a whole year of delightful stories.

Supportive parenting community

Join a community of conscious parents who seek connection with their children.

www.consciousstories.com

Andrew Newman – author

Andrew Newman has followed his deep longing for connection and his passion for spiritual development in a 12-year-long study of healing. He is a graduate of the Barbara Brennan School of Healing and a qualified Non-dual Kabbalistic healer. He has been actively involved in men's work through the Mankind Project since 2006.

His portfolio of work alongside his therapy practice includes: publishing over 1500 donated poems as the PoemCatcher, volunteer coordination for Habitat for Humanity in South Africa and directing Edinburgh's Festival of Spirituality and Peace.

Liesl Bell – illustrator

Born and raised in South Africa, Liesl moved to New York where she started her illustration career by creating corporate illustrations for IBM and Xerox's human resources intranet sites. Since then, she has had a line of hand-crafted greeting cards and illustrated numerous educational and private children's books, one of which awarded "This Book Rocks Award" for illustration. Her motto is: Create it with a smile and a wink. She now illustrates full-time in Jeffreys Bay, South Africa where she lives with her young son and two dogs.

www.zigglebell.com

32

**stickers
for
sharing**

and for your
Star Counter

Star Counter

Every time you breathe together and
read aloud, you make a star shine in the
night sky.

Place a sticker, or color in a star, to count
how many times you have read this book.